Ben's Pens

The Sound of Short E

By Alice K. Flanagan

The
**Child's
World**®

Ben has a lot of pens.

Ben counts them,
one to ten.

Ben gives a pen to Jen.

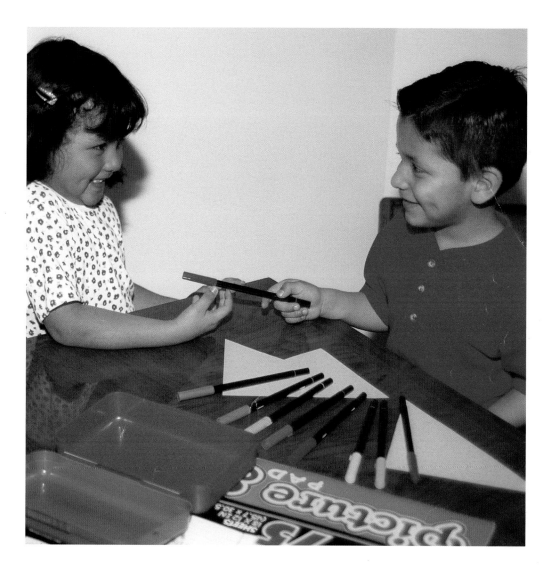

8

Jen draws a little hen.

Ben gives a pen to Meg.

Meg writes a letter
to Peg.

Ben gives a pen to Ted.

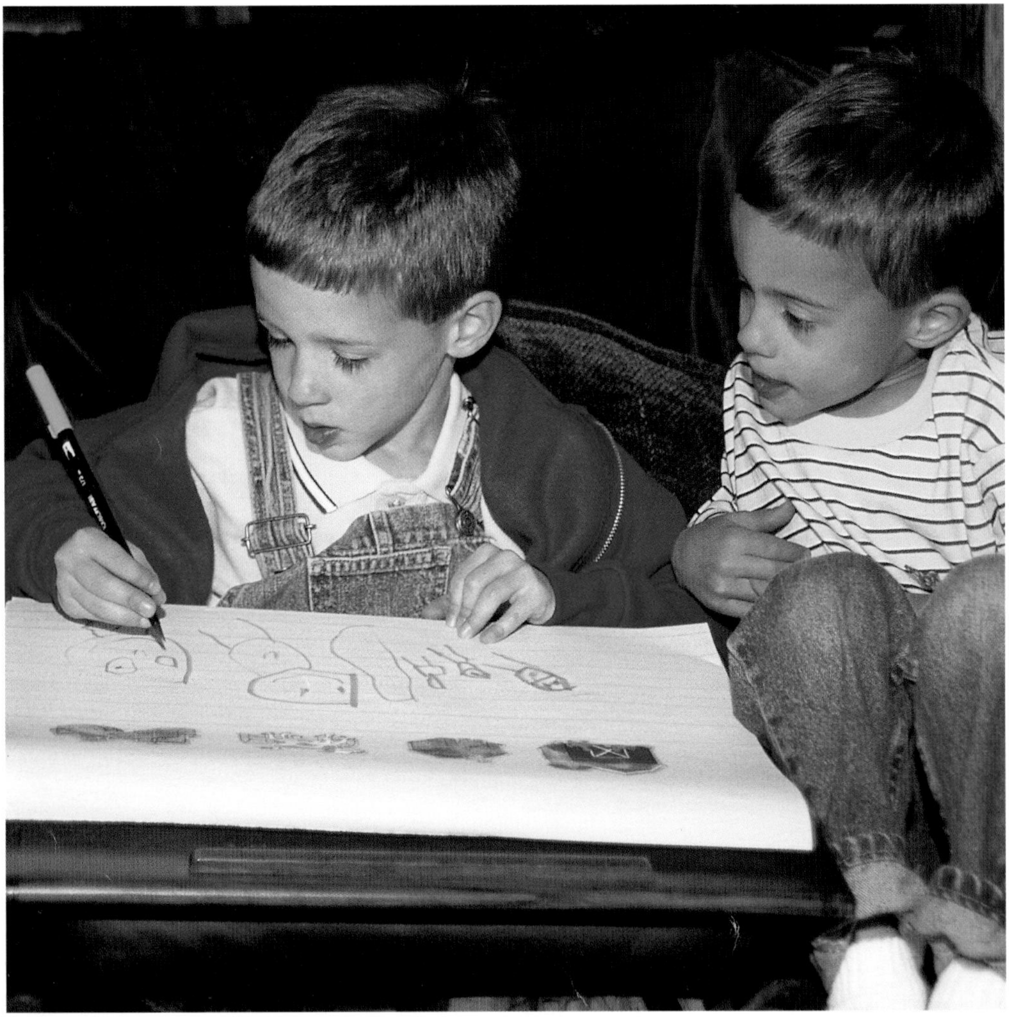

Ted makes a picture
for Ned.

Ben packs up a pen
to send.

How many pens are
left in the end?

Word List

Ben	Ned
end	Peg
hen	pens
Jen	send
left	Ted
letter	ten
Meg	them

Note to Parents and Educators

Welcome to Wonder Books® Phonics Readers! These books are based on current research that supports the idea that our brains detect patterns rather than apply rules. This means that children learn to read more easily when they are taught the familiar spelling patterns found in English. As children progress in their reading, they can use these spelling patterns to figure out more complex words.

The Phonics Readers texts provide the opportunity to practice and apply knowledge of the sounds in natural language. The ten books on the long and short vowels introduce the sounds using familiar onsets and *rimes*, or spelling patterns, for reinforcement. The letter(s) before the vowel in a word are considered the onset. Changing the onset allows the consonant books in the series to maintain the practice and reinforcement of the rimes. The repeated use of a word or phrase reinforces the target sound.

As an example, the word "cat" might be used to present the short "a" sound, with the letter "c" being the onset and "–at" being the rime. This approach provides practice and reinforcement for the short "a" sound, since there are many familiar words with the "–at" rime.

The number on the spine of each book facilitates arranging the books in the order in which the sounds are learned. The books can also be arranged into groups of long vowels, short vowels, consonants, and blends. All the books in each grouping have their numbers printed in the same color on the spine. The books can be grouped and regrouped easily and quickly, depending on the teacher's needs.

The stories and accompanying photographs in this series are based on time-honored concepts in children's literature: Well-written, engaging texts and colorful, high-quality photographs combine to produce books that children want to read again and again.

Dr. Peg Ballard
Minnesota State University, Mankato, MN

About the Author

Alice K. Flanagan taught elementary school for ten years. Now she writes for children and teachers. She has been writing for more than twenty years. Some of her books include biographies, phonics books, holiday books, and information books about careers, animals, and weather. Alice K. Flanagan lives with her husband in Chicago, Illinois.

Photo Credits

All photos © copyright Romie Flanagan/Flanagan Publishing Services

Special thanks to the Garcia family

Photo Research: Alice Flanagan
Design and production: Herman Adler Design Group

Library of Congress Cataloging-in-Publication Data

Flanagan, Alice K.
    Ben's pens : the sound of "short e" / by Alice K. Flanagan.
        p. cm. — (Wonder books)
    Summary : Simple text and repetition of the letter "e" help readers
learn how to use this sound.
    ISBN 1-56766-695-7 (lib. bdg. : alk. paper)
    [1. Alphabet. 2. Stories in rhyme.] I. Title. II. Series: Wonder books
(Chanhassen, Minn.)
PZ8.3.F6365Be   1999
[E]—dc21   99-25498
                                                              CIP